ITSY BITSY *Widow*

ANNELISE REYNOLDS

Copyright

© 2021 Annelise Reynolds
Itsy Bitsy Widow

For questions or comments about this book, please contact the author at:
authorannelisereynolds@gmail.com
Editor/Formatter: Ryder Editing and Formatting
Cover Designer: Dark Water Covers
Deposit Photos; Spider Web Graphic: @ AskhatGilyakhov
Deposit Photos: Black Widow Spider Graphic: @ macrovector

Dedication

To my parents:

Even though you will probably never see this,
thank you for always supporting me and
encouraging me to keep writing.

PROLOGUE

I watched him from the shadows as he grabbed the dancer's ass while she gave him a lap dance. She smiled and encouraged the groping like she enjoyed it, but she didn't know the man petting her up as she ground down on him to the beat of the music. She didn't know he wrecked people's lives. Would she even care? Probably not as he slid another bill into the tiny strings, barely holding together what little clothing she had on.

The rage I've held onto for two years while I finished school, a promise I made to Aunt Celeste before she died, boiled deep in my belly. It was a sickness that has festered since Daphne's death, and a vicious poison that ran through my blood until I buried my aunt beside her daughter.

Aunt Celeste was never the same after Daphne, and her death baffled the doctors. But I wasn't. She died of a broken heart, and I was left alone. I finished my last year of college barely, but I got the diploma which I immediately burned.

It was worthless to me. Years spent and money wasted because I had no intention of using it for anything anymore. Instead, I spent the last few years of school nurturing this hate and anger inside me. It was finally time for me to take my revenge and ease the rage that's been building for far too long.

When the music shifted and changed, the dancer moved away from my prey. Once she was onto her next client, I made my move. Sliding from my booth in the shadows, I moved toward the man that I was going to destroy—just like he helped destroy my family.

"Well, hello to you too." He grinned when I slid into his lap without invitation.

I smiled and leaned close as I felt his hands caress my body. While the rest of the girls were mostly undressed, I had a micro-skirt on with a sexy top that both hid and showed my body off at the same time. The boots were what made the outfit, though. I had on thigh-high boots that hugged my legs, but they served another purpose too—they hid the small vile that I was about to tip into his drink.

"Did she get you all excited?" I whispered into his ear.

"Yes, but so do you, baby. Are you going to dance for me?" He held up a twenty, and I slipped it from his fingers.

"I'm not a dancer. I work in another—related—business." I smiled coyly at him, leaving him with no doubt that I was a hooker looking for a John.

His hand slid up the exposed part of my thigh, but I tsked at him and stopped his hand before it could reach the juncture of my thighs. I leaned in close again and trailed my hand down his chest before grabbing his hand and pulling it away.

"We need to talk money first, baby." I pouted up at him. "My pussy isn't cheap."

"Hey," a voice interrupted us, "You're not supposed to work in here, sweetheart. You're taking money from my girls." The heavyset owner came over, pissed-off that I was entertaining one of his customers.

"I'm his wife." I sent the owner a smile, "We're spicing things up a little."

The man holding me agreed, and that satisfied the owner. Once he walked away, I looked back at the man holding onto me. "So, *husband*," I exaggerated the word, eliciting a grin from him. "Are you ready?"

"Fuck yeah!" He pumped his hips beneath mine, and I could feel the hardness of his cock under me. His dick would be the death of him, and he didn't even know it yet.

I cupped his face with my left hand, bringing his lips closer to mine as if I was about to kiss him. It was all the distraction I needed. He was focused on our mingling breath as I slipped the vile from my boot and tipped it into his half full scotch. He was so keyed up and ready to rut—the bastard would never see it coming.

"Finish your drink and I'll meet you outside." I got up from his lap and gave his dick an affectionate squeeze through his khakis. He downed the rest of his drink, and I smiled as walked away.

Tyler Davis was dead before I made it to my car, and I was long gone before anyone knew. One down, three more to go.

CHAPTER ONE

My heart stopped the first time the sheriff's car pulled into the driveway next to mine. When I realized he lived there, I relaxed a little. It was just my luck that the man that could catch me and put me away lived in the house next door.

"Hey, neighbor!" I looked up from the town newspaper I was reading to see the sheriff coming out his door in a pair of running shorts and a T-shirt. His big dog was on a leash, vibrating with excitement because they were on their way out for a run.

"Hi…" I said cautiously, giving him a small smile. I leaned down to pet the dog when he started sniffing at me. "Hey there, handsome."

"The dog gets a better greeting than me. I can't take him anywhere." His voiced was laced with humor, and I felt my cheeks pinken with embarrassment.

"What's his name?" I asked, trying to change the subject.

"Badger."

"Hey, boy." I smiled as I petted him. He rewarded me with a playful lick. I always thought that dogs could see into someone's soul, they could read people better than any human. I took the fact that this dog wasn't running from me or attacking me as a tell that even though there was blood on my hands, and there would be more, that deep down, I wasn't a danger to anyone who didn't deserve it. That, underneath it all, I was still a good person.

"He's adorable." I stood up, and he rubbed against my legs.

"Thanks. So, you're new in town? Are you going to the university?"

"No. Just looking for a change of pace."

"I can understand that. Welcome to Eagle Wind—" he paused, waiting for me to fill in my name.

"Rayne." I swallowed hard against the nerves of telling him my name.

"Pretty name. I'm Sheriff Dax Winchester." He held out his hand for me to take. I hesitated for a moment before letting his strong, firm hand close around mine. It was electric, like nothing I ever felt before.

I pulled away from his grasp quickly and nervously tucked the hair behind my ears, avoiding eye contact with him. He made me feel something—dangerous.

"I need to go. It was nice meeting you." I said, turning to walk back into my new home. I shut the door and leaned against it, waiting for my heart rate to settle.

I'd killed a man, and would again, but my heart didn't race the way it did in the presence of Dax Winchester. I was more nervous shaking hands with my new neighbor than slipping poison into the drink of one of the men that destroyed my family.

Sheriff Winchester was a temptation and a complication. Getting close to him would be like playing with fire, but he drew me to him like a moth to a damn flame.

CHAPTER TWO

I took a job in the local diner; the money was shit, but it gave me the opportunity to get the lay of the town and the people in it, especially the officials, since it was right across the street from the courthouse and city hall.

Being the last surviving member of my family meant that their estates all went to me. My parents, who had died when I was thirteen in a car accident, had life insurance. Money wasn't as important as being able to have part-time flexible hours that helped me be in close proximity to what went on in the city.

People tend to ignore servers when they are talking across the table. After being at the diner for just over a week, I had regulars that came in, including my neighbor. He was one of the few that walked through the door and didn't ignore me.

His eyes seemed to follow me around the room, and there was this look on his face that gave me chills, like I was a puzzle he wanted to solve. When our eyes met, I felt vulnerable and exposed.

"Rayne." His timbre was deep and soothing.

"Sheriff," I said, placing his coffee in front of him. I never called him Dax, even though he asked me to. If I called him sheriff, it kept him in a mental box that had 'do not disturb' written all over it. "What can I get for you?"

"Business as usual, I see." He grinned up at me before ordering a breakfast plate. I was about to take his menu, but he held it fast until I let our gazes meet. "You could let your guard down just a little."

I shook my head. "Not with you." I gave him a small sardonic smile. "If I gave you an inch, you'd take a mile, Sheriff. Tell me I'm wrong."

He laughed, and my belly tightened with a need and hunger that I was having a harder time denying each time I saw him. "You're not wrong, Rayne."

I took the menu from him and moved to put his order in. I grabbed the coffee pot and started making my way around the diner, refilling coffee. I was mid pour when one of the names on my list came through the door.

I knew him better than he knew himself, probably. I've combed through his social media posts and watched him from the shadows over the last few weeks. When I wasn't at home, I was lurking and waiting for the right moment to take him out. His number wasn't up yet, though. There was one more in front of him that I'd be dealing with tonight.

Professor Brant Griffith, number two on my list. He was a creature of habit, which made him easy prey. Every morning he left the house at seven on the dot.

He had classes at eight-thirty, ten, one, and two-thirty. His students seemed to like him, and why wouldn't they? From his ratings online, the girls found him hot, and overall, he was an easy professor giving students reviews that gave them test questions verbatim.

Brant Griffith wasn't married, and that was a good thing since he had an ongoing thing with a couple of different students, none of whom knew about each other. He rotated meeting the girls in the next town over a few nights a week. Tonight was student number three's night, and the perfect opportunity for me to get into his house.

There was no alarm, and the professor's house was in a quiet neighborhood, one that people would be able to see if someone who didn't belong. Lucky for me though, his house was at the back of the neighborhood, which met up with the city park.

It was nine-thirty. The park was closed and darkened, but I'd been running there since I moved here, so I knew the route like the back of my hand. I knew which house was his and took note each night when I ran just at dusk or dawn.

My car was parked at the local superstore a block away. It was time. There were a few lights coming from the houses surrounding his, but I hid in the tree, my beanie pulled low over my brow. I'd scoped this area so many times, watching the neighbors as much as I'd watched the man himself.

The couple on the right were always fighting. Their kids were in bed by eight, and that's when they couldn't stand to be in each other's company. The man would be sleeping on the couch, with the tv turned on, and the wife would be in their bed.

Like clockwork, the light in the living room went off and the low flicker of the tv light in the living room cast shadows on the curtains. The couple on the other side was an older couple. Their kids were grown, and they were already sleeping. Their house was dim except for the faint glow of the lights they left on inside. All was quiet.

ITSY BITSY WIDOW

Silently, I hopped the fence into the professor's backyard. My head was ducked low, and I stayed crouched down as I moved across the yard. I had about an hour before he returned from his bang session with student number three.

I easily got through the backdoor and into his modest home. It was too easy; he might as well not have locked the door, for all the good it did him. My gloves made sure my prints weren't left behind, and my hat hid my hair and kept any stray strands from falling.

I moved quickly and quietly through the house, using the faint light of my burner phone. When I got to the master bedroom, I found his bed unmade and wrinkled. Clothes were thrown haphazardly in the corner near a bin, but not inside, and the furnishings looked distinctly masculine.

Everything was quiet. I grabbed the spray bottle I brought with me and misted his bedding. I switched on the fan overhead to help it dry quicker as I made my way into the bathroom. After a quick look in the medicine cabinet, I found what I was looking for. I took his epi-pens and moved them into a shoebox in the closet, then grabbed all his allergy medicines and emptied them into the toilet, flushing them away.

ANNELISE REYNOLDS

Brant Griffith was highly allergic to nuts. His bedding was now laced with a light coating of peanut oil that he'd be breathing in all night long. If he caught the scent when he laid down, it would be too late. His medications were gone, and his emergency epi pins were in a place he'd never look.

I took the time I had to go through his side drawer. Luckily, I found another epi-pen hiding there. I wanted him to have no way to escape. He would die, slowly, a little at a time while his throat swelled closed.

On my way out, I turned the modem to his internet and home phone off, just slightly disconnecting the wires. The only thing I had to worry about was a cell phone, so I went into the laundry room and hid a low powered cell phone jammer inside a box of powdered laundry detergent. The signal would be blocked from within the house, but not much further.

By morning, I'd have the second name marked off my list.

CHAPTER THREE

"How's Badger?" I shouldn't be provoking conversation with the Sheriff next door, but God, I couldn't help myself.

Dax gave me a tired grin. "Probably pissed I haven't taken him on his run yet."

"You look tired, Sheriff." I let my eyes run over his body. He was still in uniform, though his shirt was untucked, and his utility belt was slung over his shoulder. The metal from his cuffs glinted in the fading sunlight at me. It was sobering to see them there.

"Long day." He responded with a shrug of his shoulders.

"If Badger would let me, I could take him on a walk for you," I offered with a light shrug.

Dax stopped and studied me for a second before he gave me a playful grin. "I'm beginning to think the way to your heart is through my dog, Rayne."

I leaned my head back on the headrest of my rocking chair and sighed. "My heart isn't worth trying to get into anyway, Sheriff. Don't think it's more than it is. I've never had a dog to walk, and you look like you need a shower, food, and sleep, not necessarily in that order. I was just trying to help and get a small piece of a life I've never had by walking a sweet dog. That's all. Trust me, I'm not worth your time or effort."

I watched from the corner of my eye as he ran his fingers through his hair and scratched at the day's stubble that covered his jaw. "How about you walk Badger with me? It's been a rough day and I could use the company."

It was reckless to engage the man. But a part of me—the small part of me that was still alive deep inside, couldn't say no to him. He was a brief glimpse of normalcy, an image of what I knew could never be. My path was set, there was no going back from the road I was on, but maybe there was a small glimmer of light along the way, like Dax and Badger.

"Okay," I whispered around a knot in my throat. I knew I shouldn't tempt fate. My words would be guarded, and I would have to give him just enough to satisfy his curiosity about me, but not enough to hang myself and end up with iron bracelets. Not yet, at least.

Dax entered his home, and I could hear the happy barks from Badger as he greeted him at the door from the seat on my porch. He was gone a few minutes and came back out wearing a pair of basketball shorts, a T-shirt, and running shoes. He'd changed for our walk, and Badger was happy on his leash, ready to take off running at the first sign of clearance from his owner.

"He looks happy." I smiled, getting up from my seat and moved toward the happy duo. When I got close, Badger greeted me with his excitement, jumping and putting his paws on my belly. Standing on his hind legs, his head reached my chin, and I loved him for it. "Hey, buddy. You ready to go play?" I pet him and rubbed his ears, greeting him with affection and putting a kiss on his head.

My eyes met Dax's over Badger's head. He had a soft grin on his face, but he looked away and muttered under his breath. I swore he said something about being jealous of his dog, and I hid my smile and stepped away from the excited pup. "May I?" I asked, holding out my hand for the leash.

"He's strong," Dax warned, as he handed me the lead.

"I think I can manage, but if not, I know the owner." I gave him a flirtatious, lighthearted wink and took the loop from his grasp. Our fingers brushed and electricity zinged between us.

We set off walking down our street. A few people waved at Dax and looked at me curiously.

The ones that did wave called out, and he responded with each of their names. Nobody knew me, and I was okay with that. Hell, I never even would have known Dax if the man wasn't the Sheriff and didn't live right next door to me.

"So, why haven't you ever had a dog?" He finally broke the silence when we reached the stop sign at the end of the road. Badger took his time inspecting it before lifting his leg and peeing on the grass around it.

"I don't know, honestly. Guess it was just never in the cards for me. My parents died when I was young, and I lived with my aunt who was a single mom herself." I gave him the basics of my background without going into full detail.

"I'm sorry to hear that. Having a dog as a kid is a lot of fun. You get all the good without any of the responsibility."

I let out a soft chuckle. "Isn't that how it is for most children? Everything good in life without the responsibility that comes with being an adult."

"If you're lucky." He shrugged. "I was lucky, but some aren't. Some kids have to grow up way too soon."

"I'll agree to that," I said, stamping down the ice and panic that tried to flood through my veins. "Did you grow up here?"

ITSY BITSY WIDOW

I knew the answer. I'd done my research on my sexy neighbor when I found out that the town sheriff lived right next door. You know what they say, keep your friends close and your enemies closer. While Dax wasn't exactly my enemy. Yet, one day, he would be. There would be a blue line separating us, him on the right side of the law and me on the side of the lowly criminals. He'd have no choice but to hunt me down, and I'd have no choice but to let him.

"Yes. I was going to leave once upon a time, but fate intervened. I guess it thought I needed to stay."

"What happened?" I asked as Badger pulled me along to the next stop on his marking every inch of territory he could path. It was kind of comical. I didn't realize dogs had such big bladders.

"I was playing football and blew out my arm before I could go pro." He shrugged like it was nothing, but to an athlete, I knew it wasn't nothing.

"That sucks," I murmured. I knew exactly what it was like to have the world ripped out from under you unexpectedly. His was physically taken from him. Mine was an emotional tsunami that tipped my world over and turned me into what I am.

"Yeah. Life happens, though." He shrugged again. "I'm not unhappy being sheriff, but it wasn't my first choice for the path I wanted to take."

"You can always change your path." Ironic coming from me, but Dax had options I didn't. He didn't have blood on his hands and a vendetta to make right. If he wasn't doing something that made him happy, then he could find something that did. "If you weren't sheriff, what would you do?"

He gave me that half sexy, cocky grin that I liked so much. "You mean if I'm not playing ball or being sheriff?"

I rolled my eyes at him. "Yes. What would be your first obtainable option?"

"Before I signed on as sheriff, I thought about being a coach for the high school football team, but they weren't hiring."

"Did you look outside of Eagle Wind?"

"No. Not really." He laughed at himself softly.

"You gave up too easy."

"What about you?" he asked. "I know you don't want to be serving coffee forever."

I shook my head. "Forever's not really an option for me, so for now it will do."

I wished I could take it back the second I said it, but he slipped in and I let my guard down. "Are you sick?"

"I'm not ready to talk about it, Sheriff," I lied, letting him believe that I was sick.

In a way, I was sick. Not many people can plan out and execute a kill. Most people—good people, don't have the stomach for something like that, but I was fueled by a rage so deep I could barely contain it.

"Rayne."

I shook my head and cut him off.

"No," I said as I thrust the leash into his hand and took off running back home—back to the safety of the shadows and the web of lies my life had become.

CHAPTER FOUR

I avoided Dax for the next week, but I watched him coming and going from the safety of my house. A few times, I thought he saw me lurking in the window upstairs, watching as he left in the morning or came home in the evening.

He would look toward my house like he wanted to come over but didn't know whether or not he should. Part of me wanted him to, but I knew it was better if he didn't. I was already starting to feel attached to him. He drew me in with his cocky, flirtatious grin.

Dax Winchester was charming and good. The darkness that dwelled in me longed for the lightness he offered. I couldn't trap him. I couldn't bring him down with me because there was nowhere else for me to go.

I sighed and looked at the empty house around me. I didn't have much furniture. I didn't need it. I had six months left in this house. No more than that. It was almost time for me to take down my third target, he was the riskiest of my victims because he was the one most often surrounded by people who weren't drunk, and by now, he was aware that the two men he had crossed a line with were both murdered.

Chad Philips was mayor of Eagle Wind, Washington. Getting in to have a meeting with him put a record of your visit on the books, so that was out. I needed to get to him another way, but he wasn't like Tyler, visiting seedy strip joints and cheating on his wife. He wasn't even like Brant, his schedule varied from day to day. He went home to his family each night, and he had no deadly allergies I could exploit to end his life.

As far as I could tell, Chad Philips was a decent husband and father. Too bad he made a fatal mistake when he joined up with his friends and gang raped my cousin. They were responsible for sending her to drugs and alcohol before she ended it all. She hated herself and couldn't live with the memories of what they'd done to her anymore.

I know. I opened the suicide letter she'd dropped into the mail before she pulled the trigger. She'd sent it to me, telling me everything. There were splotches of bleeding ink from where her tears fell as she wrote her final words to me.

They destroyed Daphne. She was a beautiful soul before she left for school. When she came home to Southern Cali, she was a changed person. She no longer cared about school, all she wanted was to get drunk. Eventually, the alcohol turned into drugs, and Daphne turned into a shell of the person she was before. My best friend was gone, and I had no idea why until after I received her letter in the mail.

After and Celeste died, I was all that was left. My family tree was down to a single stump—me. There was no blooming from that. The only thing that kept me going was the rage and anger I felt toward the men that destroyed my family. With each name I marked off my list, I felt a little lighter and a little darker at the same time.

Everything about my life was a lie. I lived for the sole purpose of righting the wrong that led to the death of what was left of my family. The doctor's said Aunt Celeste had a heart attack, but I know she was never the same after Daphne. She died of a broken heart, and I'd see to it if it was the last thing I did, that Chad Philips and his father both paid for the part they played in death of my family.

"You've been avoiding me." I looked up to see Dax getting out of his personal truck.

"I have," I admitted. There was no use in denying something so blaringly obvious. I made sure I wasn't outside when he came home from or left for work until now. Over a week had passed since our walk with Badger.

"Why'd you run?" He leaned against the side of his truck as we talked.

"You know why," I answered softly, my dark eyes meeting his hazel ones.

"You're sick." He said it like it was a matter of fact. "What do you have?"

"Nothing that can be cured," I replied. Sick was relative. To someone who couldn't fathom taking the life of another human being, then yeah, I was sick.

"How long do you have?" He swallowed hard, emotions playing across his face.

I shrugged. "It doesn't matter, Dax. I'm not worth losing sleep over. I'm not worth getting attached to."

"I hate that you feel that way."

I leaned my head back, closed my eyes, and died a little inside. Why hadn't I met him before? Why hadn't Daphne met him when she'd been up here? I could have accepted anything, even them getting married if it brought her back and made him happy. He was a genuinely good guy, and

ANNELISE REYNOLDS

I—I was caught in a dangerous game of lies, deceit, and death.

There was no room in my life for a good guy, which made me feel like shit for trying to use him to get close to the mayor, but The Eagle Wind Wine and Dine Charity Event was the best shot I had at getting close to the mayor without detection.

I felt bad for lying to him, bad that I had to use him, and let him believe the worst. My future was death by fate, not circumstances I created with my own insatiable anger. Killing the men on my list didn't faze me. They were evil and deserved what they got, but lying to and using Dax made me feel shame and regret, and it made me wish for a different life.

The event was held every year at the Wild Wind Country Club, and the town's upper crust attended. I'd seen pictures of Dax in a tuxedo when doing my research on the previous year's event. If that man was hot in his uniform and street clothes, he was devastating in a tux.

He rubbed shoulders with a few people I recognized from my sporadic shifts at the diner, including the mayor himself. They didn't seem to be friends though, not from the gossip I'd been able to pick up from around town and the research I'd done into the Mayor and Dax himself.

The Mayor's wife was once Dax's fiancé, but shortly after his football chances ended, she ended the relationship. The stupid woman had no idea what she'd given up with Dax, all for a man that had taken the innocence and life from a young girl because she'd ended up at the wrong party they happened to be attending. She was an opportunity.

No, there was no love lost between the Mayor and Dax. Their cordial relationship was superficial at best, but they were both public figures in the community, and that ensured they needed to work together.

"Life sucks sometimes."

"That it does." He gave me a rueful smile. "It's a nice night. I was going to fire up the grill and throw on some steaks. You want to join me?"

I swallowed hard at the line that I was about to cross with this man. "It depends," I said softly, playing the part of the scared girl I used to be.

"On what?"

"You. No strings, Sheriff. If anything happens when I walk through that door with you, there can be no strings, because we have no future. I need you to know that."

CHAPTER FIVE

The steak was cooked to medium, the company was good, and everything seemed perfect. I didn't have many perfect moments in my life, but this definitely fell into that category. We talked about music and movies as we sat in the two Adirondack chairs he had on his back patio.

He had an old chewed up tennis ball that he kept throwing into the grass for Badger to chase with the dog's ears flopping wildly in the wind. I enjoyed the moment, knowing full well I wouldn't have many of these left.

"I haven't eaten that good in a long time." I smiled, my eyes closing as I felt the soft breeze settle around us in the cool evening air.

"What do you normally eat?"

I shrugged. "Whatever I can get in a bag most of the time. I don't cook much, but I can make a mean bowl of Spaghetti-O's."

"Oh, look at you. A regular Emeril Lagasse."

I laughed and stretched out a little more in the chair.

"You want another beer?" he asked.

"No. I'm good." I barely finished the one he'd given me, and I didn't need to get tipsy around him.

It was fully dark by the time I decided to go home and get some rest. He would not invite me to go with him tonight, and that meant I needed to try to think of another way to get an invitation out of someone.

I stretched, feeling the muscles in my back and shoulders flex and tighten. "I better be getting home before I fall asleep in your chair." I yawned and pushed to my feet.

Dax followed suit, standing up beside me. I only came up to his shoulder, and just being near him sent pulses tripping through my veins. I looked up at him in the faint glow of the outside light. We didn't say anything, our bodies just moved toward each other.

Our lips met softly at first. Fear and anticipation swirled within me. I couldn't quite catch my breath as the kiss deepened. My body warmed and shuddered at the same time beneath his touch as he pulled me closer to him.

"Wait," I said, not moving from his embrace, just stopping the progression momentarily. He raised his head, looking deep into my eyes. Questions lingered there, along with need and desire. "I want you," I finally said, admitting to both of us out loud that I felt more than I should—wanting things I couldn't have.

"I'm not going to stop you, Rayne." He gave me that crooked little grin I was falling so hard for. "I want you too."

"Only this once," I said, grasping for anything I could to remain in control of the storm swirling inside of me. "Only for tonight. I can't promise anything else."

"Then we'll have to make tonight last a lifetime."

Dax captured my lips in another kiss. This one was harder and more desperate. His tongue danced with mine as he pulled me closer against the hard length of his body. I felt the evidence of his desire against my belly and swallowed hard.

"Come with me," he whispered against my lips, backing away and taking my hand, leading me through the back door. Badger followed behind us, and when we went inside his townhome, the layout was exactly like mine, only his looked like a welcoming home instead of a cold, empty house.

The decor was manly, basic, and traditional. Not surprisingly, the living room housed the biggest TV known to man. I looked at it and laughed. "Is it big enough?" I asked jokingly.

"Oh, it's big enough, even when turned off." He gave me a grin and a wink, and I laughed at his double entendre. Nerves fluttered in my stomach, and a glimmer of happiness was just out of reach. I was tempting myself with what could never truly be.

Daphne was on drugs before she died. One taste was never enough. She was always looking for her next fix. I knew that one night with Dax was going to be my drug. I'd take my hit, and I'd have to live with the memory of it until my revenge was complete and my plan was done.

We went into his bedroom. The massive bed took up most of the room. As soon as we passed the threshold, he closed the door with Badger on the other side.

"Your dog will be mad at me for taking his place in bed tonight," I said ruefully, looking at the door.

"He'll get over it. If we only have one night, I plan to make the most of it. Come here." He pulled me back against him and our lips met as he walked us backward toward the bed.

When he pulled his lips from mine, he started kissing his way down my neck. I rolled it to the side to give him better access. His hands started pulling at my clothing, undressing me. My pulse thickened and my core liquified. I could do nothing but hold on to his shoulders and feel the waves of need crashing through the air around us.

"Fucking beautiful," he said, pulling back long enough to get my shirt over my head, exposing my simple black bra covered breasts.

My chest heaved as I tried to catch my breath. We'd only just started, and already I felt like I'd run a mile. He did that to me. I wished I'd met him before, but there was no going back from where I was.

He kissed me again. I shivered at the heat of his body and the feel of his hands on my bare skin. Dax removed my bra easily as our mouths melded together and our bodies danced against each other in a pseudo sexual dance. We moved, trying to get closer, eager to get to something deeper that would satisfy us both.

Dax's lips left mine and moved downward, nipping and kissing along the way. When his lips closed around the hardened peak of my breast, I moaned and threaded my fingers through his hair, holding him close as his mouth tugged at the sensitive bud.

"Dax…" I threw my head back, calling out his name. It felt amazing. His lips went from one breast to the other and my hips rocked against him with every tug on my nipple. I needed more. I needed it all.

ITSY BITSY WIDOW

I felt his hands unbuttoning the fly of my jeans. When he had them opened and unzipped, he guided me to lie back on the bed. I did, my hips pressing against the edge of the bed as he went down on his knees beside me.

We didn't talk as he removed my shoes and what was left of my clothing. I sat propped up on my elbows as I watched him place kisses along my belly. I sucked in a sharp breath when his tongue flicked inside my belly button and when his teeth scraped across the skin just above where my jeans had rested.

Dax guided one of my feet onto his shoulder, opening wet slit to his hungry gaze. "You're so wet," he said, tracing a finger down my sensitive eager flesh.

I collapsed back on the bed when his tongue met my damp, needy flesh. His tongue was incredible. When he pushed his fingers inside me, I flinched, and he froze.

"Rayne?" His voice was hoarse as he choked out my name. Dax's eyes met mine again when I sat up. My face was heated. I'm not sure if it was in need or embarrassment that he'd discovered one of my secrets.

"You're my first," I confirmed softly. Boys had never been a priority for me in high school. I thought they were childish and self-centered.

When I went to college, it could have happened, but I wasn't there long enough before my destructive cousin came home. I was too focused on not taking her path that time got away. Then Daphne died, and I learned the truth. There was just no time and point to a relationship. Especially after I lost Aunt Celeste.

I lost everyone I ever loved or who loved me, and eventually I would lose Dax too. It wasn't a matter of if, but when. When he found out who I was and what I've done, there would be no forever. There was only now.

He leaned his head against my thigh, his eyes closed, "How am I supposed to let you go?" His voice was rough with emotion that I didn't want to put a name to.

"You won't have a choice, Dax."

His eyes met mine before he nodded sadly. He placed another kiss on my mound before slipping his fingers out of me and standing to his feet. I watched from my position as he licked his fingers clean, then started removing his own clothing.

"Get back on the bed." He instructed notching his chin toward the center of the mattress. I scooted back, watching as each of his rippling muscles was exposed. When he pulled off his jeans and boxers, I sucked in a sharp breath. He was huge. I hadn't been wrong in my estimation when I'd felt him through the layers of our clothing.

I swallowed hard as he stroked the long length of his cock before climbing on the bed with me. "I'm clean, Rayne. I had a test after my fiancé cheated on me, and I haven't been with anyone since. Are we protected?" he asked, his eyes boring into mine.

"Yes," I lied. I never planned for this—for him. Of everything I planned out, Dax blindsided me, but we only had one night, and I didn't want to feel anything between us physically. There were so many secrets there already, that I just wanted to be connected to him in some way.

He moved over my body and kissed me again. Our lips met in a hungry, erotic dance. I felt the heat of his shaft at the apex of my thighs and it made me writhe with need. I wanted more.

His fingers traced down my body and moved between us. He shifted slightly to guide the head of his shaft to my opening. I bent my knees up, going by need and instinct, opening myself to him wider.

I felt the head of his cock brush against my clit, and I gasped at the jolt of pleasure it sent through my body. When he started adding pressure, my body resisted his intrusion at the same time I desperately sought it. It was a wild riot of emotions.

"God, you're so tight, Rayne." He groaned when the thick head of his cock started to finally inch its way in. "Feels so fucking good."

I couldn't talk because it felt good. My pussy was stretching around him, like a stiff muscle that you haven't stretched in a long time. It feels painful but so good at the same time.

"Dax," I said, wriggling under him, "just dive in."

"I don't want to hurt you." His jaw was clenched like he was fighting to hold on to his control.

"I don't break that easy, Dax. I want you. For tonight, I'm yours. Take me that way."

He leaned down and kissed me, absorbing his weight on his forearms, so he didn't crush me. I felt him move in small thrusts, but with each forward push of his hips he sank in a little deeper. When he met the resistance of my virginity, he pushed all the way through.

I broke our kiss and gasped at the pinch of pain, but it didn't last long as my body adjusted around him. When he started to move, that pain morphed into something else entirely.

So, this is what love felt like. A tear slipped from the corner of my eye as the emotions of what was happening crashed over me. Every minute I spent with this man, I fell a little more in love with him, and I knew I'd betray him.

My heart broke at the same time it sang with joy. I needed a distraction from the pain in my heart, so I threaded my fingers through his hair and brought his lips back to mine as we rocked together. I felt my core coiling tighter and tighter, and I knew it wouldn't be long until I felt the release I'd only ever heard about.

Stories didn't do it justice. My body bowed up against his, and I tore my lips away as I cried out and another tear escaped. I felt my body pulsing around his, grasping at him—milking him. When he groaned, I felt a flood of heated seed fill my passage. God, I wanted more, but it was dangerous for me to want what I knew I couldn't have.

Dax pulled me into his side, my head laid on his chest and our legs were entwined as we caught our breath.

"When are you going to tell me?" he asked quietly. The fan above us was the only other sound in the room besides our breathing.

I closed my eyes and put my forehead against his chest. I'd lied enough to him, but I didn't want to tell him I was sick in a way that would make him hurt more. That seemed too cruel. I couldn't make him feel that kind of pain.

"I promise, you will know soon. Can that be enough?"

"You're not giving me much of a choice in it," he ground out. I knew I was making him angry by holding back.

"I'm sorry, Dax. I didn't plan for any of this. I need a few more days, maybe a few more weeks."

"If I have to wait for answers, I will, but I want something in return."

I propped my chin up on top of his chest, "What's that?"

"Another night."

"Dax," I said, knowing it was a huge mistake, but also knowing exactly what I felt was returned. I loved him. Somehow, I fell in love with the Sheriff next door. I didn't even think I was capable of love anymore.

"There's this charity event I have to go to next weekend." He twirled a section of my hair around his finger. "Give me until then. Let's have this week."

"That's just going to prolong the pain, Dax. It will make it harder to walk away, for both of us."

He kissed my forehead, "Good. I don't want either of us walking away. Not yet."

I should have said no, but there were two things holding me back. One, I wanted my week with him. I wanted the love of my life for as long as I could have him because he would hate me soon enough, and two, he'd just given me the invite I needed to get close to my next victim.

"Okay, one week."

CHAPTER SIX

Pictures of Dax in a tux didn't do him justice. He looked like he just walked out of a magazine when he came to my front door.

I smiled and raked my gaze over his body. A body I've gotten to know carnally over the last week. We made love every night when he got home from work, and on his off days, we barely left the bed.

If I wanted to pick up shifts at the diner, I did it when he was on duty. Most of those days he came in for either breakfast or lunch to visit me. It was tempting, being normal. Dax gave me a small glimpse of what my life could have been if things were different, and I had to keep reminding myself that it wasn't.

"You look—wow," he said. His eyes gave me an appreciative once over.

I wore a simple, elegant, formal, off-the shoulder- black dress that hugged my body. It had a slit up to my thigh that showed off my leg when I walked. My red clutch gave me a pop of color, but the most important part of my outfit was the ring I wore on my finger.

"Thank you." I smiled. "You too."

He held out a hand for me and pulled me against him, giving me a hard, quick kiss. "How the hell am I supposed to keep my hands off you?"

I laughed and leaned up for another quick kiss before I whispered, "You're not."

He groaned and took my hand, leading me out of the house. "Woman, you're going to be the death of me." I flinched and lost my footing, but he caught me.

"Sorry," I said, blushing a bright red.

"Easy. You okay?" His brow furrowed with concern. I just nodded and gave him a small smile. I shouldn't have been so nervous, but I was. This was unlike my previous kills. The mayor would be surrounded by people, his wife would be at his side most of the night. I had to get close enough to him without raising suspicion, just in passing, long enough for me to use my ring to take him down.

"I'm good. I haven't worn heels in a while." I gave him the small excuse, which was true, but not the reason my step faltered. "Let's go."

Dax could dance. I was surprised to find out that my ex-football playing sheriff had some pretty decent moves on the dance floor.

"Where did you learn to dance?" I asked as he spun me around the floor. I hadn't seen the mayor come in yet, so I was relaxing and enjoying the time I had with my date.

"I took some classes in the city when I was in college."

I laughed, surprised. "Why? That doesn't seem like something most guys do."

"It's not, but that's also why I got all the girls." He winked at me. "I went to a lot of events and had a lot of dates because I knew how to make my way around the dance floor."

"I bet you didn't need the moves to get dates." I shook my head. He was too charming and perfect. He would have had no trouble getting girls.

"No, but it also made me a higher commodity on campus than the next guy."

The music changed from a faster beat to a slower, more melodic tune. Dax pulled me close against him, and I rested my head against his chest. There were a few other couples on the floor with us, but everyone else was milling around talking and sipping on champagne.

ITSY BITSY WIDOW

When the slow tune ended, we moved off the floor hand in hand. Dax had just taken two flutes of champagne from a passing server when I saw him come in. Chad Phillips, number three on my list, came in with his wife, followed closely by number four.

I felt the change coming over me. The rage that seemed to calm down when Dax was around bubbled slowly to life, knowing that they were here. I had one chance to make this happen, so I had to wait for my moment and take it.

CHAPTER SEVEN

It was hard to focus on his movements without being obvious that I was watching for my moment to strike. Blue octopus' venom had taken out Tyler. I'd used Brant's own peanut allergy to poison him. Chad would die by the prick of a pin coated in golden tree frog venom.

He would never even know he was pricked, let alone poisoned, I just had to wait for him to head toward the bathrooms. It was almost nine when I got my chance.

"Hey, I need to use the ladies room. Afterward, you want to head home?" I gave Dax a heated look. The dinner had been wonderful, the music was great, but I was ready to get him out of his tux.

"Yes." He gave me a smile and kissed me. I hurried across the room, weaving through the crowd of people. When I got to the back hallway, I saw the mayor coming toward me. I gave him a smile before I "lost my footing", faked this time.

He caught me and never even realized I'd pricked his hand with a pin in my ring.

"I'm so sorry." I said, feigning embarrassment.

"It's alright, Sweetheart." He gave me a cheesy grin.

"Thank you. I must have had more to drink than I thought." I gave a little giggle to excuse my clumsiness.

"Drinks can sneak up on you."

"Yes." I gave him another small smile. "Enjoy the rest of your li-night." I giggled again and went the rest of the way down the hall to the bathroom. I went into the stall and threw the ring down the toilet, flushing it away.

Before I left the bathroom, I took the replica ring from my purse and slid it onto my finger. I waited a few more minutes before leaving the stall and going to the sink to wash my hands, scrubbing them hard as if to clean the remnants of what I'd just done away.

Meeting my reflection in the mirror, I noticed my dark eyes were laced with a pain buried so deep that it was hard to recognize myself. It was second nature to hide behind my walls. I was an expert at it, but I couldn't live this way forever. It took a lot to keep yourself hidden inside, to keep the rage buried in your chest and not combust from it. I had no desire to hurt an innocent person. The men I killed; they were far from innocent.

Dax was the only bystander in all of this, and his pain would be emotional, not physical. I just hoped he could eventually move on from the pain I knew I was going to cause him.

I looked in the mirror one more time, and turned away, as a small group of women came into the bathroom. They weren't talking about the mayor yet, so I knew he hadn't collapsed. It would be soon though. The pin had been laced with enough poison to take him down.

When I walked back into the ballroom, I searched for Dax. I found him waiting by the exit doors, talking to number four on my list. The interaction looked intense, and I almost thought better of approaching the two men.

Almost. "You ready?" I smiled at Dax as I approached them, giving them just enough time to end their discussion.

"Absolutely." He offered his arm, and I slipped mine inside. "Enjoy the rest of your evening, Charles."

"What was that about?" I whispered when we were out of ear shot?

"He's telling me how to do my job but won't tell me why he's suspicious in the first place."

"Don't you think you should consider what he says? After all, he was the sheriff before you."

Dax looked at me, "Maybe. I'll call him next week and schedule a meeting, but if he can't give me anything concrete, I have to go off what the ME says."

We were almost to the front doors when a flurry of activity picked up. There was a commotion in the ball room.

"Shit," Dax said and threaded his fingers through his hair in frustration. "I've got to see what's going on. Grab a chair and give me a few minutes." He kissed my head and took off running back to the ballroom.

I took a seat on a sofa in the lounge. The luxurious leather allowed me to sink into the comfy couch. When the ambulance came, sirens blaring, I knew it was too late. The mayor was dead, and my night with Dax was over.

CHAPTER EIGHT

The mayor had a big funeral service. Dax had to go as part of the city staff. I found out he didn't care for the guy, but he would go pay his respects.

"I never thought the uniform would do it for me, but you definitely do it for me no matter what you wear." I smiled, seeing him get into his dress uniform for the funeral.

"I have to go to work afterward. I'm sorry I won't be back until late."

"It's okay. I'll figure out something to do." I smiled, already knowing full well what I was going to do today.

I went to the front door with Dax, only wearing a sheet from his bed. We made love last night until I couldn't move anymore, and my body ached in the best possible way.

At the front door, he pulled me close, his hands slipping inside the sheet and loosening it. I stood naked in his embrace as he kissed me deeply. That ache I felt was nothing compared to the need for more of him.

"Do we have time?" I whispered against his lips.

He chuckled and looked at his watch. "Only a few minutes if I don't get undressed."

"We can work with that," I said, opening his belt and letting his pants fall with the weight of his equipment.

Dax pushed me against the wall and speared into my welcoming heat. There was no need for foreplay, I was already melted and ready for him. His hands and hips pinned me to the wall as he pounded into my silken flesh.

It was fast and hot. Fireworks exploded behind my eyelids as my toes curled and the orgasm zinged through my core. I cried out his name and pulled him close, savoring my time with him because I knew it was coming to an end.

I was waiting in his house when he got home from the funeral. He knew I was there before he saw me. His cop instincts must have told him he wasn't alone.

"I know why you're here," he said into the darkness before flipping on the light.

I was sitting on one of the stools at his kitchen island, facing the door, a gun hiding at my back, a recorder hiding in a plant on the coffee table.

"I figured you would, Sheriff Philips." I called him by the name he'd taken for granted. Someone had come to him for protection and justice and he'd turned her away, running her out of town because it would compromise his family. "Ask anyway."

"Did you kill my son?"

"I was just another drunk girl in a hallway, Sheriff." I shrugged, not outright admitting it.

"You were with Dax last night."

"I was. He's a good guy—good sheriff." I paused. "A hell of a lot better than you were."

"I won't disagree with that. What do you want?" He took his jacket off and threw it on the back of the couch. He looked old and worn out like he'd aged twenty years in the last three days.

"My cousin back, but that's not going to happen."

"So, she's dead?"

"Yes. If she hadn't ended her own life, the drugs and alcohol would have eventually killed her." I bit out the words like acid. "When she came home, she was a totally different person, and we didn't know why. I didn't find out until I got her suicide letter in the mail."

ITSY BITSY WIDOW

I got up from my spot and picked up the gun. "Your son and his friends didn't just destroy one life that night, Sheriff. You would have been better off sending them to jail than running my cousin out of town when she went to you for help."

"He was my son!" he shouted back at me, but I didn't flinch. I remained in control, this was almost over, and I could finally be free of the rage inside me. The pressure had released little by little, and I was ready to feel lighter.

"And he raped my cousin with his buddies because she dared to show up to a college party and drink too much," I spitefully said back to him. "When she came to you, what did you tell her?"

He didn't answer me, so I pulled the gun from my back holster and pointed it at him. "What did you tell her, Sheriff?" I asked again, holding the gun steady.

"I don't remember what I said." He clenched his jaw that was covered with gray whiskers.

"Here, maybe this will refresh your memory." I handed him the letter. "Read it."

The old sheriff took the letter from me and opened it. I'd read that letter so many times over the last few years while I planned this, that I had it memorized. "Read it out loud," I insisted when he didn't start right away.

"Hey Rayne, I'm writing this letter because I can't take it anymore. I can't take what they did to me. The highs I get only relieve the pain and the shame for so long." He stopped reading and swallowed hard.

I picked up where he left off, "I needed one person to know the truth about me. About them."

"Stop," he said, closing the letter, unable to look at it anymore.

I didn't stop, like his son didn't stop and his friends didn't stop that night when my cousin cried for them to. I recited the rest of the letter from memory.

"I went to Sheriff Philips the next morning. But when I got there, he already knew what his son and his friends had done." I paused and cocked my gun. "What did you do, Sheriff?" I asked him again.

He didn't answer, but I waited. Guilt and regret washed over him, "I offered her a tissue then put a rag covered in chloroform over her mouth."

"Don't stop there, *Sheriff*," I said the title with derision and all the hatred I felt. "What happened next?"

He shook his head, refusing to say the rest.

ITSY BITSY WIDOW

"You injected her with heroin while she was out." My control was slipping, my hands starting to shake. "You told her nobody would believe a junkie and that you would plant drugs on her if she didn't get out of town." I summarized the rest of it. "She came to you for help, and you destroyed her even more than your son and his friends already had."

"I protected my son," he ground out.

"And now he's dead, along with his two friends, my aunt, and my cousin. Was protecting him worth all the lives it cost, Sheriff?"

"He's my son."

"Yeah. And he's waiting for you." I pulled the trigger, aiming right for center mass. Just like the guy at the shooting range taught me. The makeshift suppressor muffled the sound of the twenty-two as I fired three rounds into his chest.

EPILOGUE

The guard guided me down through the white walled hallway to visitation and sat me down in a room with a glass partition and a phone. It was something like out of a movie, as I waited to see who was coming to visit. I had no family or friends.

The only person I could possibly see coming for a visit was Dax, but then again that was unbelievable too. He probably hated me right now, and I couldn't blame him. I killed four men. Each of them deserved what they got, but that's not something a good man like him would ever understand or take lightly.

I swallowed hard when I saw him sit down across from me. My heart was in my throat, and my eyes ate up the sight of him. I missed him already. Was avenging my cousin and my family worth it?

Before I met Dax, I would have said yes without hesitation, but he changed me. It just happened a little too late. I was a thousand miles down a path that there was no coming back from by the time I met and fell in love with him.

Seeing him through the glass and not being able to touch him was the harshest punishment within the prison walls.

We didn't pick up the phones right away, we just stared at each other. He looked like he hadn't been sleeping well, and I couldn't say I had been either. He was still the most gorgeous man I'd ever seen, though. His dark hair was a mess like he'd been running his fingers through it.

When he reached for the phone on his end, I grasped mine. My hands were shaking, and my stomach rolled with nerves. I felt like I was going to be sick.

"Hi," I said, breaking the silence between us. It was barely more than a whisper, but he heard it.

"You asked me to come."

I did—weeks ago, but I hadn't heard anything from him since the day he testified against me at my trial. That's the last time I saw him. The anger and hatred I felt rolling off his shoulders, it took everything in me not to react.

"Yes," I said, biting my cheek so hard that I tasted blood. This would probably be the last time I ever saw him.

"What do you want, Rayne?"

"You weren't part of my plan, Dax," I finally said, desperate to get him to understand. "I didn't plan to move and be your neighbor. Everything that happened between us, that was all chance. I never intended to hurt you."

He nodded dispassionately before looking away, "Is that it?"

"No," I weakly replied. The moment of truth had arrived. He had heard my whole story in the trial, and the conversation that happened between me and Sheriff Phillips that I recorded before I shot him dead. He knew what they had done to my cousin. How the three of them had gang raped her.

They had read her suicide letter that she'd mailed to me before taking her own life at the trial.

Dax knew that the previous sheriff had failed at his job protecting my cousin. He had run her out of town, forcing her to deal with being raped on her own, and feeding her the drugs that were the fucking catalyst that started her own downward spiral. She tried to live with the pain, using drugs and alcohol to cope with the ghosts haunting her until she put the barrel to her head and pulled the trigger.

The circumstances of my cousin's death, and the grief over my aunt's death shortly after, took the death penalty off the table for me, but I was supposed to be serving four life sentences. One for each life I took. I would die in this prison, I knew that. Hell, I knew that going in. It was no surprise.

Dax was the surprise I never intended on. Our baby was the surprise I didn't see coming. My heart ached that I would never know our daughter.

"I have something to ask of you, Dax, and I wanted to be the one to tell you and ask it."

"I don't owe you anything, Rayne." His words came out bitter and cold, but I didn't blame him.

"I know that. Trust me, I know. But what I'm about to ask you, involves you too."

"What?" His jaw clenched tightly, and I knew he was holding onto his emotions by a thin strand. I could see it in the set of his mouth and the way his shoulders were taut with tension.

"I need to know if you will take care of our daughter." I laid the phone down on the table and stood to the side, smoothing out the orange jumpsuit so he could see the bump underneath.

I was just over three months along. At the last ultrasound they told me it was a girl, and I cried. I cried for my cousin, my aunt, myself, and the path that my life turned down. I cried for the fact that if Dax wouldn't raise our daughter, then she'd end up in the system because I had no family to care for her.

Shock washed over his face. He set the phone down and stood up to pace. He paced from the wall back to the desk and back again. I stayed sitting, waiting for him to adjust to what was happening. I've had weeks to deal with this, and he didn't.

When he walked back over to the table in front of me and picked up the phone to speak, I swallowed at the despair I saw in his eyes.

"Was any of it real, Rayne? Was anything between us real?"

I swallowed hard and tried to stop my tears from choking me, but I couldn't. "You were the only thing that was ever real. Everything else was a part I played, but you were real. If I could take it all back for a chance at a life with you, I would." Tears filled my eyes, and I pleaded that he understood how much I truly did love him.

"I'll take care of her," he finally said, hanging up the phone.

I nodded, got up, and walked away from the love of my life. I didn't turn back, and after my daughter was born, there would be no going forward.

I finally understood the pressure and confliction my cousin must have felt in those final moments before she made the choice to take her own life. It was a choice I decided to make, too. I had already made it before Dax showed up to talk to me. Once our daughter was born, I'd be following my cousin down the same path, ending my miserable life so that my daughter and Dax won't have to deal with the betrayal and heartache that comes with loving a murderer. It was the only way I could see any of us truly being happy. The second I made that first kill, my chance at a happily ever after ended. I was nothing more than a poisonous spider who had woven a web of endless lies—a web neither of them should've fallen into.

Yes, I may have forfeited my own happily ever when I took another person's life, but it eases the pain in my heart to know that when I take my final breath, the man I love will be holding our daughter on the outside, showering her with the love I only wished I could give her, and raising her to be someone I'll never be.

Someone good. Someone honest. Someone exactly like him.

The End

ANNELISE REYNOLDS

Acknowledgements

I have so many people to thank for this book.

First and foremost, my babies. My kids sacrifice mommy time (trust me that's a big deal to them), so that I can write. When I'm on a deadline and it's tight (which is how it's been the last year), they know that my focus has to be on getting the words out. I am so very blessed to have my Little Miss and my Little Man. God knew I needed you both in my life. Thank you for being the amazing, beautiful souls that you are.

This life can be a crazy place to navigate, but with the help of some amazing women, I know I have a killer circle I can depend on. Thank you: Vanessa Kelly, Dawn Sullivan, S.L. Romines, Amy Jones, Tracie Douglas, and Taylor Dawn. You ladies are amazing, and I'm so very blessed to have you all in my small circle. You guys are the absolute best.

Speaking of the best, Quinn Ryder, my amazing editor who deals with my crazy ass and my last-minute rush edits. I don't know what the hell I'd do without you. Thank you so much for all the hard work you put into each of my books. You make my words far prettier than I can do on my own, and I greatly appreciate you and your family for not killing me when I drop things on you at the last minute. Love ya much, woman.

Tracie Douglas, thank you for this kick ass cover. I bought it a few years ago from your premade group, and when I saw it—it spoke to me. I knew the story I wanted for it, but I didn't know when the opportunity would present itself for me to use it. When Heels, Rhymes, & Nursery Crimes came along, it was the perfect fit.

Lastly, to my ARC team, my fan group, and my readers at large. I couldn't do what I love without your continued support. Thank you so much for giving me a way to live out my dream. You are all truly amazing. Thank you.

 A

Other Books by Annelise Reynolds

Standalone
Ridin' Nerdy

Steel Demons MC Series
Phoenix Bar

Ember's Burn

Holiday Heartthrob Series
Bidding on Santa

Stupid Cupid

Christmas Calamity

Love & Fireworks

Volkov Bratva Trilogy (SRS)
Nikolai

Viktor (Coming Soon)

Konstantin (Coming Soon)

Author Bio

I spend my days working, my evenings with my two wonderful kids, and my nights are when the characters in my head are given free rein. The tagline for Phoenix Bar, "Beauty After the Burn", holds special meaning for me and really helped to give birth to the story. Like Phoenix, I've had to rebuild my life from the ashes. It's been a long journey with a roller coaster of emotions and stresses, but I can truly say where my life is now is more beautiful than where it was. I am fulfilling my lifelong dream of being an author.

Made in the USA
Middletown, DE
17 August 2021

45466757R00040